LAZY JERIAH

LAZY JERIAH

TALIN KOCHKRIAN YAKOUBIAN

Lazy Jeriah

1603 Capitol Ave., Suite 415 Cheyenne, Wyoming USA 82001

+1 307-316-1175 |Readers Quill Agency LLC

Published in the United States of America

ISBN 978-1-970617-52-8 (Paperback)
ISBN 978-1-970617-56-6 (Hardback)
ISBN 978-1-970617-53-5 (Digital)

Chapter One

A long time ago, the king and queen had only one daughter, and her name was Mazel. It was a wonderful day with a blue sky and a warm breeze. Mazel was standing on a balcony of the castle looking out over the city. Her long, golden brown hair flew out behind her as it got caught in the breeze. The soft curls fell all the way down to the backs of her knees. Her eyes were one of her more interesting features with one eye blue and the other green.

Mazel's personality was unique. She was always lonely, quiet, and persistent. She would much rather sit and read books or help the needed people of the city rather than attend royal functions. One day when she was going out from the city to the village, her parents caught her taking merchandise and food from the castle to give to the poor people of the village. Mazel had done this more than a dozen times before, but now her father, the king, was furious.

"This is the last time that I'm telling you," he said. "You are not to take things from the castle, and go out into the village. Behave, or I will marry you off."

He turned in a swirl of red and green robes and marched back into one of his council chambers. The flock of diplomats eyed her suspiciously before following suit. The big, heavy, wooden door creaked shut and slammed decidedly.

Mazel stood there all alone as she let her father's words sink in. He had been trying to marry her off for the past three years, but each suitor he brought before her had been turned down. Much to her father's dismay, Mazel always found something wrong with the men. He was either too good-looking or not good-looking enough; his breath smelled bad; his beard was a mess; he was either too pompous or too soft-spoken.

In reality, Mazel didn't want to get married. It never really crossed her mind because she was so happy living in the castle. She had a lot to live up to, being a princess and all, but she didn't want to just settle for whichever man could offer her father the best price. She would rather be alone for the rest of her life than be stuck in a loveless marriage, and she was happy to help the people in the village.

Dressed in a long, white tunic with a velvety robe tied over it, the king paced his bed chambers tirelessly. His wife, the queen, sat up in their luxurious bed with the covers already pulled over her lap. Her long, black hair had been plaited and hung over one shoulder while she looked over some documents by the light of a candle. A small fire was burning in the fireplace, mostly to light the room rather than warm it.

"I just don't understand Mazel," the king said on one of his passes in front of the bed.

"What's to understand? She's young and thinks she knows everything about the world even though she's barely been outside of the palace walls. In time, she will come to understand what her duty is to us and her kingdom."

"Her kingdom?" the king asked. He stopped and looked at his wife with lowered eyebrows. "The kingdom is far from being hers yet. If I can't trust her to pick a husband, how can I trust her to run an entire realm?"

The queen put her papers to the side and looked her husband in the eyes. “Don’t you think you’re making too much of this?”

“Absolutely not.” The king picked up his pacing again and cinched his robed tighter around the waist. “She is too headstrong for her own good. If we let her carry on like this much longer, no man will want her anyway.”

The queen laughed and got out of bed. She walked over to her husband and put her arms around his waist to make him stop moving. “Dear, she’s a beautiful, young woman, and any man would be pleased to call her his own.”

“Well, then soon she’ll be too old. She should have been married last year.”

The queen looked away, and the king took this moment to make his case more clear.

“We’re running out of time. She needs to marry and produce some heirs. She needs a king to rule with her, and I think I have a plan to make her see my way.”

The queen pulled back. The king had a faraway look, but his mouth was turned up in a smirk. The queen knew exactly what that meant, and it wouldn’t be anything good for Mazel.

“I think she needs to learn a lesson.”

“A lesson? What kind of lesson?” The queen walked back to the bed and got back under the covers. She was already exhausted and hadn’t even heard her husband’s plan yet, but she knew it probably wouldn’t be anything she wanted to hear. She placed the papers on the table by the bed and blew out the candle.

“She needs to learn what it is like to truly struggle in life.” The king stared into the fire as the plan began to form in his mind. “She needs to learn that there are worse men out there for her to marry than the ones I have offered to her.”

The queen didn’t say anything, but it was another hour or so before the king finally let the embers of the fire die out before he crawled into bed beside his wife. He fell into a deep sleep, satisfied with the plans he had made and would put into action the following morning. If Mazel wasn’t married in time, she would not be able to take over the kingdom, and the king’s cruel brother would inherit everything. The king was not going to let that happen.

Chapter Two

ife out in the village couldn't have been more different from life in the palace, especially for one man named Jeriah. He had short, brown hair that curled around his temples and kept a close-shaved beard. He was of average height and blended in with a crowd.

As he was growing up, his family had never been wealthy, but his father had done well enough to always keep the family gratified. Jeriah had loved his parents tremendously and looked up to his father as a hardworking, friendly, and humble carpenter who taught him the trade. Jeriah's mother was just as hard working around the house and always had an offspring love and caring for Jeriah.

When Jeriah was only nine years old, his parents were invited to a wedding in a village a couple days' trip away. They each gave Jeriah a kiss goodbye and said, "We will see you in two days, son." They knew Jeriah would be able to make it through the night without them but also trusted their neighbors to step in if he needed any help. Jeriah waved happily as he watched their cart drive away. He knew he would see them soon.

Jeriah waited for his parents to come home two days later. He knew they wouldn't be back until late in the evening, so to surprise his parents, Jeriah decided to make dinner for them. He knew they would be tired from their journey. He made an easy stew his mother had shown him. He knew he would be able to complete it on his own.

When it was almost dark, Jeriah began to grow anxious. He went outside and sat on the doorstep as he watched for the cart. Unfortunately, when Jeriah's parents were

coming back from the wedding, they were waylaid by robbers who killed them for their goods and stole their camel.

Jeriah waited and waited for his parents to return. He sat outside of the house all night and watched down the road for any glimpse of their arrival, but they never came. He never went back into the house and left everything as it was. He refused to go back inside even when his stomach growled incessantly. He was on his own then.

It had been a scary time for Jeriah to live on the streets growing up, hardly moving from the house. He didn't have anyone he could rely on, and all of his possessions and food came from donations. He didn't want to get a job. He had seen his mother and father work so hard for all of their lives, but that didn't stop somebody from taking their lives and the goods they had worked so hard to get. That was how he got the name Lazy Jeriah. He slept most of his days and refused to get a job.

Chapter Three

he walk into the city was quiet, and he didn't run into many people. He knew a place where he could usually talk himself into a warm bowl of stew and immediately headed that way. The bread and apples had been good and filling earlier in the day, but now Jeriah's stomach felt empty. He did have a few coins if he couldn't talk the cook out of a bowl or two, but he wanted to save his money. He knew there would be a few games he would be able to get in the next day, and he needed money to put down.

Jeriah had to duck his head to get through the doorway into the cook's house. This place of business was only open at nights, and the meal usually consisted of the day's leftovers thrown into one big pot. This was why the cook was usually willing to just give a bowl away to Jeriah. Otherwise, it would go to waste.

"Evening, Jeriah," the cook called as Jeriah took a seat near the fire.

"Evening, John," Jeriah said in return. "What have you got cooking tonight?"

"Oh, nothing special really. Mostly vegetables that were about to go bad, but I had some good spices left that I threw in for good taste."

Jeriah looked around the room. There was only one table with a couple of stools, and an old couple sat there with their bowls of stew pulled close. Sometimes the place got rowdy if some men happened to stumble in after drinking heavily, but tonight, it was quiet.

"Slow night?" Jeriah asked.

John narrowed his eyes and folded his arms over his chest. "I'm doing all right."

Jeriah held up his hands in defense. "No, that's not what I meant. It's just quiet is all."

John laughed, and the old couple looked up for just a moment. "Go on and have a bowl."

"Thanks, John. How much?" Jeriah made to take out his money but moved slowly. He was sure that John would stop him.

As predicted, John said, "No charge tonight." He ladled a large helping of stew into a bowl and placed it in front of Jeriah. Then he bustled around and began to clean up his cooking area.

Jeriah relished the warm broth and the soggy vegetables. There were chunks of meat though he couldn't tell what animal they came from. John had been right about the spices. They added the perfect amount of flavor. John's fare was usually lackluster, but tonight's was probably the best Jeriah had ever had, and it really filled him up.

Jeriah had been hoping for more people to be there that night. He didn't really like spending time by himself that much because that was when he truly reflected on his place in life. He lived a fairly easy life and could come and go as he pleased. He didn't answer to anyone, but he also didn't have a place to call his own. He didn't have a family to go to at the end of a long day, and that made it difficult. Focusing on that wasn't something he enjoyed.

Jeriah stayed there for a few more hours talking with John who eventually gave Jeriah a second bowlful of stew. Eventually, John told Jeriah to go home because John was ready for bed. John didn't know that Jeriah was homeless, but he knew was poor, and Jeriah didn't offer the information. He liked John well enough for a good meal, but he didn't think it would ingratiate him to beg for a bit of floor to sleep on.

Instead, Jeriah took his pride back out on the street. By now, it was completely empty. Everyone had gone home to their families or was so tired from work that they had collapsed on their beds in sleep. Jeriah was still wide awake after his refreshing nap that afternoon. He wandered around the empty streets with no destination in mind.

Even though he was all alone, Jeriah enjoyed getting to know the city while it was empty. He knew which areas were safe to sleep in and which he needed to avoid. He was looking for an easy life, and he had become good at begging and gambling. Besides, he felt as though it was too late to make something else of himself. He had spent so many years learning this particular craft that he felt like he would be completely useless as a farmer or a carpenter.

Jeriah walked past the palace but barely glanced up at the imposing walls. It wasn't in him to wonder what went on behind those gates or to dream of what life would have been like had he been born rich. It didn't really matter much one way or the other to him. He finally found a barn that looked relatively empty. He knew the owner in passing. He knew a lot of the city folk through his years on the street. He figured if he were caught, the owner wouldn't be too hard on him, so he looked around before slipping through the crack in the door, careful not to make a sound.

He was right. The barn was relatively empty. There was a horse and a donkey, both of which barely moved as Jeriah took careful steps into an empty stall. It was clean with fresh hay that he fluffed up into a suitable bed. It was probably close to midnight when Jeriah closed his eyes and fell asleep.

Chapter Four

The king was in a much better mood than day before. He went through his daily work of listening to petitions from the city folk and sitting through meetings with the lesser lords of the region. One was upset because no one could get water. It was a strange occurrence where anyone who went down into the well to see what was happening never came back again. The whole town was growing sick from lack of water, and the diplomat wanted something done.

The only thing the king could think to do was to order the surrounding towns and the people in the surrounding countryside to offer their water to the city people.

"I promise to send someone to investigate this further," the king said before adjourning the meeting. He had more personal problems to take care of and a plan to set in motion.

The king moved to a smaller chamber with only his closest advisors. He wanted to make sure some of the officials were on board with his plan before he really got into it. One wrong step could cause the city to rise up against him, and that was the last thing he wanted. He learned through his years as king to keep the officials in the loop, and they were less likely to get upset about it. They really just liked to be included.

Once everyone had settled in their seats, the king raised his hand to quiet them down. "You all are probably wondering why I asked you here, and I promise to make this brief. Most of you are aware of my daughter, Mazel, and her particularly picky ideas concerning marriage."

Several of the men in the room chuckled. Mazel's headstrong attitude was infamous within the palace walls though most of the city people thought she was a beautiful and poised young woman.

"I think I have a plan to make her see the error of her ways and finally settle down."

There was a glint in the king's eye that nobody in the room could miss. A couple of men sat forward in their chairs, eager to hear more. Mazel's resistance to marriage didn't just plague the King. The councilmen were also worried that she might not marry in time. No one relished the idea of the king's brother taking over the kingdom. He was known as a cruel man. But more than that, no one wanted such a headstrong woman to rule over them. They didn't know what kind of chaos she would cause in their meetings or changes she would want to make. It was something they didn't want to think about.

No, it would be much better for her to have a husband for them to deal with. They needed to find a man who would put her in her place.

"My daughter needs to learn a valuable lesson before she can take over the kingdom. She needs to learn what life will be like if she continues on the path she is headed down." The king licked his lips and rubbed his hands together. "I want to find the laziest man in the city and marry her to him."

Silence fell across the room as the king's plan sunk in. One man was stroking his beard in thought, while another one just looked confused. Finally, the oldest man in the room with wispy white hair spoke up. "How will this teach her?" he asked.

"If she sees how awful a common man will treat her and what it is like to struggle, then I think she'll better appreciate the privilege she has grown up with. She has never had to work or struggle a day in her life. I know that her stubbornness will get the best of her in a marriage like this."

"And how will you force her to marry this man? You haven't been able to force her into a marriage yet," another man spoke up. "And how will we know he's the laziest person in the village?"

"I haven't quite figured that out, but I can threaten her and the life of this other man. I don't think she will want to be responsible for some man's death."

There was murmuring now among the diplomats. "Why didn't you just threaten her before with a better suitor?"

The king let out a loud and long laugh. “I can’t threaten the life of a prince or young lordling. That would be cause for war. But I can easily threaten and execute some no-name without anyone batting an eyelash.”

The general of the king’s soldiers spoke up, “I have an idea to find the laziest man in the village.”

When he told the king his plan, the king immediately agreed. There were no more questions as the councilmen realized the king was serious and probably not one to mess with. He was right though, no one would care about the safety of some random peasant picked off the street. Chances were no one would notice the urchin had even disappeared. Everyone felt sure that this plan would work, and there was no way Mazel would want to stay married to some lowly man with no prospects.

Before the king adjourned the meeting though, one of the younger men cleared his throat and asked, “What if she wants to stay married to this man after all? Are we going to allow some common man to become king?”

The king leaned forward in his seat. He was raised higher than the others in the small room and already looked menacing. “Trust me,” he said without room for argument in his voice, “she will want out of this marriage.”

The men adjourned except for the general.

“I expect your plan to work,” the king said. “I want him to be poor and unskilled. Bring him here to me, and let no one see you bring the man in. That is of the utmost importance. You may go. Come find me when you have found this man so I can see him. And I repeat, let no one see you bring him here.”

“Yes,sir.”

The general turned on his heels and immediately left the chambers. The king sat back in his luxurious chair and smiled. He was sure that this plan of his would show his daughter the right way—his way.

The following day, the general went out on the front steps of the palace and proclaimed to the village people, “All lazy townspeople must meet tomorrow morning by the river. Anyone who doesn’t attend will be punished. Don’t say you didn’t hear.”

He sent out soldiers all around the city and village to proclaim this message and to ensure that every single person heard the message. On Sunday morning, every lazy person attended except for one. Only Jeriah didn’t attend because he was so lazy he didn’t want to move. He wouldn’t get up and walk to the river even with the threat of punishment.

But the soldiers found him and brought him to the river along with the other lazy men. "All right," the general said, "everyone needs to swim as far as you can go to the other side and come back again."

The men started groaning, but the soldiers began to push them closer to the banks. The men started swimming, including Jeriah. When they reached the other side, they all started to swim back, except for Jeriah this time. He wasn't used to this kind of work and was too lazy to come back. He started to drown, and the general ordered one of the soldiers to jump in and save him.

"All right, you can all leave," the general said when Jeriah was thrown up on shore. "Except for you." The general pointed down to Jeriah who was lying on the ground out of breath.

Chapter Five

azel had just woken up to the bright sunlight pouring into her bed chambers. Her bed was so soft, and she wished to just turn over and dive headfirst back into the dream she had just had. She had dreamt that she was on an adventure in some faraway, exotic land where she met a handsome man who fell madly in love with her. It was a common theme of her dreams, and she wasn't quite ready to face her reality.

But she was a princess and had things to do. Her breakfast was already laid out, so she tumbled out of bed and stumbled over to the small table covered with pastries and fruit. Mazel looked out of the window and over the tops of the village to the fields beyond. She had never been that far but had always wanted to go. *What is over that mountain?* she wondered.

Mazel had just taken a large bite from a fruit pastry when her mother walked in unannounced. It wasn't surprising; the queen didn't like to fuss with formalities when it came to her daughter. Instead, she blew in like a leaf on a breeze and immediately began to go through Mazel's wardrobe.

"Good morning, Mother," Mazel said after she had swallowed her food. "What are you doing here so early?"

"I am picking out an outfit suitable for today's events," the queen said.

Mazel walked over and watched her mother rifle through her things. "What's going on today? Nobody mentioned anything yesterday."

"It has come on quite suddenly."

Her mother hadn't yet looked at her, which seemed strange. Mazel tried to crane her neck, but the queen was doing her best to look the other way.

"Okay, what's wrong? What have I done now?" Mazel asked as she plopped down on a chair.

"Nothing, honey, you just need to look your best today."

"Why won't you look at me?"

The queen stopped what she was doing and slowly turned around. Her eyes were red and puffy. There were black tracks down her cheeks from where the tears had washed out the eyeliner the queen wore every day.

Mazel jumped up and ran to her mother, pulling her into a tight hug. "Why are you crying?"

"It's your father. He has something planned today." The queen wiped her eyes. "I'll be fine, but you need to get dressed so we can get going."

"Can't we sit and talk about this first?"

"No, we must get going." The queen reached in the wardrobe and pulled out pleated, purple silk gown with a floor-length A-line skirt and a soft, round neckline. The sleeves, made of a lavender linen mix pattern, were a three-quarters embellishment cuff that had a butterfly shape. "Put this on."

It wasn't optional.

Mazel did what she was asked and didn't ask any more questions. She was worried about her mother and didn't think being defiant would help matters. It was one of her favorite dresses, and the purple looked stunning with her hair, while the gold made her skin glow. Her mother began to brush Mazel's long locks.

"Perfect," the queen said before she led Princess Mazel out of her room and down the winding hallways.

"Where are we going?" Mazel asked, but the queen didn't respond. It was a long trip through the palace in silence.

The queen finally stopped in front of a door. Mazel wasn't familiar with this part of the palace. These rooms were usually reserved for small committee meetings or hearings. The queen stood there for just a moment as she took several deep breaths to gather herself.

"Should we knock?" Mazel asked.

"No." The queen shook out her hands and plastered a smile on her face before opening the door.

"Ah, they're here," the king said as the two women walked through the door.

The room was barren. There were no pieces of furniture and no tapestries on the walls. There were only a couple of wall sconces bathing the room in muddy light. Three men stood in the room, however. The king stood tall and off to one side as he gave the queen a light kiss before tucking her arm in his. One man was older, but Mazel didn't recognize him. He was dressed in all black and had a long white beard. The third man was close to her age, but his hands were bound before him. His clothes were neat and clean, but he clearly didn't come from money.

Mazel could only wonder why her presence was needed. This seemed to be a trial for the young man, and Mazel didn't know who he was.

"Good morning, Father."

"Good morning, Mazel. I hope you slept well last night," the king replied. He had a huge, devilish grin on his face.

"I did." Mazel looked around the room again. The young man was also looking at everyone gathered there with confusion. They seemed to be the only two who didn't know what was going on. The queen still had her fake smile fixed on her face. "What's going on here?"

The king clapped his hands in excitement. "Just step right over here, Mazel." He ushered her across from the young man. The man in black stood between them. "You're getting married today."

Mazel laughed. "I'm sorry, but I believe I didn't hear right. I'm getting what?"

"Married."

"To whom?" In shock, she looked at her parents incredulously.

"To this young man, of course." The king pointed to the man with his hands bound.

"I don't even know him. I'm not going to marry him." Mazel turned to the bound man and said, "Though I'm sure you're a lovely man, but I'm not going to marry you."

The king's eyes flashed dangerously. "You will do as you are told. I have indulged your ridiculous notions of falling in love and put up with your defiant attitude for long enough. It is time you learned your place in life. I have found you a husband, and you two will marry."

But Mazel wasn't likely to go down without a fight. She had no problem standing up to her father in this. "I won't do it. You can't force us to get married."

"I am the king, and I can do as I wish. You will marry, or you will be disowned, and this man will be executed."

"What?" Mazel and the young man said in unison.

"You can't execute him!" Mazel shouted.

The king towered over his daughter. "If you marry him, then I won't have to."

"Please, Your Majesty, please have mercy. I'll do whatever is asked of me," the man pleaded.

"Then marry my daughter." The king turned to Mazel again. "You don't want this innocent man's blood on your hands, do you?"

Mazel felt her world shrinking right in front of her. She couldn't believe this ambush. Her parents were going to force her to marry a man she didn't know. She thought she had been in control of her life. She knew it exasperated her father every time she turned down a suitor, but she thought, in the long run, that he was on her side. She thought, eventually, he would see her point of view about marriage, but this felt like betrayal.

She couldn't stand the thought that this man's life hung in the balance either. He was clearly innocent in all of this, and Mazel never dreamed that her determination could prove fatal for somebody else. She didn't have a choice. She had to go along with this.

"Fine," Mazel said. Her whole life hung on that tiny word, and her world would never be the same.

"Excellent."

The ceremony was short and to the point as the man in black went through the marriage vows. Through everything, Mazel learned that the young man's name was Jeriah. His bonds weren't cut until they were pronounced man and wife. They both stood there awkwardly wondering who they had just married.

Chapter Six

As soon as the ceremony was finished, the queen ordered a servant to go to Jeriah's old house and clean it before the newlywed couple was to arrive. The servant prepared lunch for the couple and left before they arrived.

The somber group arrived at the cozy house just as the servant was exiting. Jeriah hesitated on the threshold. He hadn't been in this house for so many years and wasn't sure he could enter it now. But one glaring look from the king made him take that dreaded step inside.

Mazel looked around the space. She was happy to see that it was clean and a decent size, but it didn't compare to the palace. "What about my clothes and my books?" Mazel asked. "What about food?"

"Your things were brought over here already, and there is food in the cellar that should last you for a while, but you will need to make your own money to buy supplies after that." The king looked pleased with himself, but the queen remained silent. Mazel didn't dare plead with her mother though, not when her father was being so unreasonable.

"But what about the kingdom? How am I supposed to keep up with what is going on in the palace out here?"

"When I think you are ready to handle the responsibility, you will be invited back to the palace and learn your role as the future queen. But until then, you will live here with your new husband and learn a thing or two about hard work and what your place in life truly is."

The king had slammed the door shut after him, and Mazel didn't bother running after him. She wanted to cry and scream. She wanted to yell at the heavens and tell the world how unfair this was. But she didn't. She was a princess, and she knew how to behave, but she didn't know how to act with this man—her new husband.

He was a fairly attractive man, she had noticed, but she literally knew nothing about him besides his name. She didn't know if he's a cruel man or a loving man. Would he treat her with fairness? What was his family like? What were his likes and dislikes? Could this man read or did he have some other skill?

Jeriah began walking around the small house. As he walked through each room, he was flooded with memories. Jeriah remembered how his mom cooked and took care of him. He never thought he would return to this place, with or without a wife. There was a front room with chairs and a table and a separate room with a bed and a wardrobe. He found the door that led to the cellar and couldn't believe how much food was down there. He was in heaven.

When he came back upstairs, Mazel hadn't budged. Jeriah took one of the chairs and leaned back on the legs before asking, "Are you really the princess?"

Mazel crossed her arms over her chest and narrowed her eyes at him. "Yes, I am. Who are you?"

"I'm Jeriah, your new husband apparently." He was grinning like he had just won a lottery, and in most ways, he had.

"Yes, but who are you? Where do you come from, and what do you do?"

"I come from here and there. I do this and that."

Mazel was frustrated with his vague responses. "What about your family? Where are they?"

"My parents died when I was nine. As for the rest of my family, I don't know, and I don't care." Jeriah leaned forward and the chair fell onto its front legs with an echoing thump. "So am I the prince now?"

Mazel was caught off guard. Jeriah was so flippant about the death of his parents and the whereabouts of his family. she honestly didn't know if he were now considered a prince. And she didn't know what to think or what to do. Instead, she just walked away to look at the rest of the house while she collected her thoughts.

She was distressed to see there was only one bed. She couldn't share a sleeping space with this man she didn't know. What had her parents been thinking when they arranged this? Were they trying to teach her a lesson? Maybe she could go to the palace in the morning and beg them to annul this marriage. She would do whatever they asked of her after this.

She found the cellar as well and went down to see what kinds of food were there. She found a board with some cheese, grabbed a couple of figs, and a loaf of bread before heading back upstairs. She placed the food on the table and began to cut slices of the bread and cheese. “Are you hungry?”

“Famished. They didn’t feed me all morning,” Jeriah said as he took a fig and popped it whole into his mouth. “Can you cook then?”

Mazel looked up at him and gave him a half smile. “Not really. Can you?”

“I usually eat on the run so cooking isn’t typically involved.”

Mazel was starting to think she was missing something important and went back to questioning. “So what is your trade? What kind of work do you do?”

Jeriah chewed his food slowly and carefully as he tried to figure out how to word his response. He didn’t think she would take it well if he outright told her he was a vagrant, and that he hated to work. “I’m a bit of a negotiator.”

“That isn’t a title. What are your skills?”

“I am a people person. I like to make connections throughout the city and relate to people.”

“Again, that isn’t anything. What are you not telling me? Do you even have a job or a trade?”

He couldn’t talk his way out of it. “Not exactly, but as there is very little need for a princess, you don’t have any trade skills either.” He leaned back in his chair and let it sink in.

Mazel felt flustered when she couldn’t come up with a witty response to him. She had skills that she had learned as she was groomed to be a royal, but she honestly didn’t know if they were applicable to actually making money from. She knew how to dance and play music. She could draw and paint. She was learned in reading and mathematics and could even chart the stars. She knew a bit about diplomacy and national policy, but what good would that do to put food on the table once their stores ran out.

And this man before her was already infuriating. He didn’t even seem to care what they were going to do. As she thought more about it, he had really gotten the better end of the deal. He was now married into royalty while she had married below her and definitely not for love.

“I’m going to bed. You should find somewhere else to sleep,” Mazel said as she stood up from the table and dusted crumbs from her dress. She walked to the bedroom and closed the door behind. She even locked it before taking a deep breath to steady herself. She looked through her wardrobe to see what her family had brought for her and saw many outfits, but most of them were much plainer than she was used to wearing. They were clothes fit for a common woman, not a princess.

Mazel resignedly put on a coarse nightgown and slipped in the lumpy bed. It was a far cry from her luxurious chambers in the palace. "In the morning, I will find my father and beg his forgiveness," she promised herself before turning over and falling asleep.

Out in the front room, Jeriah was in paradise. He finished off the cheese and bread before he grabbed a blanket from a trunk and made a comfortable bed on the floor. There was a fire and a roof over his head. He had a comfortable blanket to sleep on and a beautiful woman in the next room that was now his wife. To top it all off, he hadn't been executed that morning.

This was a good day.

Things were just as tense up in the palace where the king and queen were sitting down to a late dinner. The only noise came from the clanking of plates and cups as the couple ate in silence. The king was pleased with how well his plan had gone, but the queen was furious at him for having sent away her only child.

"This is ridiculous, love. You can't ignore me forever," the king said after draining his glass of wine. A servant immediately showed up to refill without a word.

The queen looked up at him and then focused back on her meal. She took small precise bites and counted how many times she chewed to keep herself from exploding at her husband. It wasn't working that well, and she didn't know how long she would be able to keep her thoughts and feelings to herself.

"Dear, you must understand that what I did was necessary. She needs to learn her place and a bit of humility. I am concerned for her as well, but she is an adult now. She will come home begging for my forgiveness soon, trust me." It was a phrase he had been repeating over and over to his wife and his advisors.

"How could you do this to me?" the queen asked. Her voice dripped with hurt and anger. "How could you marry off my only daughter like that? A mother looks forward to this day, and you just snatched it away from me."

"You're upset because you didn't get to plan an extravagant wedding?" The king laughed, and it echoed around the large dining room. "You'll have your chance once this marriage is annulled."

"It is more than that. I didn't even get to make a proper goodbye to her or give her any of the advice that a mother should give to her daughter about what it takes to be a good wife. It wasn't a joyous occasion as it should have been, and we will all remember that forever."

For the first time, the king looked concern. His smile fell for the first time that day, and it suddenly looked at his wife with new eyes. Maybe she was right to some extent. Maybe he had robbed his wife of this festive moment, but he had a kingdom to think about. She would still get her chance when Mazel's marriage to this beggar was annulled, and she was properly married to someone of her own class.

No, he had to stick to his decision and watch it play out. He was still certain that Mazel would return within the next day or two, pleading with him to let her come home. She would see how hard life was out in the city and that the king was just doing what he deemed best. Then the queen would no longer be angry at him either, and they would all be able to plan a real wedding.

Everything would work out, the king was sure of it.

Chapter Seven

When Mazel woke up in the morning, she had a change of heart. She still was weary of Jeriah, but she had decided to not go to the palace to beg her father to return. The king was trying to teach her a lesson, and Mazel decided to follow through. She would stay in this house with her new husband and find a way to live. Maybe she would actually enjoy the freedom it would provide her.

She quickly got dressed in one of her plain dresses and went out into the front room. "Good morning," she called to a still sleeping Jeriah.

Jeriah didn't answer; he just turned over and pulled the blanket over her head. Mazel couldn't believe it. The sun had been up for a while already, but he still wasn't getting up. Mazel had never known anyone to sleep so long into the morning.

"Come on," she said and nudged Jeriah with her foot. "The morning is passing, and we have work to do."

"I don't do work," Jeriah mumbled from under his blanket. "Let me sleep."

Not ready to deal with him, Mazel made herself some breakfast. She had had an idea overnight that she could weaving blankets or carpet to sell. She had developed quite the eye for patterns, and her weaving were neat and tiny. She could weave, and then Jeriah would be able to take them into the city or one of the other villages to sell.

Mazel looked through all of the cabinets and trunks but didn't find anything she could use just yet. She would have to go down to the market to find some materials she could work with. She didn't have much money, so she would have to bargain with the sellers to get what she needed. She had to hope that Jeriah would be able to sell enough of it to make a decent profit for them to continue with this business.

Jeriah still hadn't moved when Mazel left the house. She made her way into the village and began looking through all of the merchants' stalls to find what she needed. Many people were friendly, and a few recognized her as the young woman who was always handing out food and clothing to the poorest people living on the streets.

When Mazel came across one stall, she was instantly greeted. "Mazel, what are you doing out here?"

"Oh, hello Abraham. I'm doing a bit of shopping."

Abraham leaned close and whispered, "What could you possibly need that the palace doesn't have?"

Mazel looked away. "I don't live in the palace anymore. I'm married now and live out here in the village."

Abraham's brows knitted together. "Who have you married that you would need to live out here?"

"His name is Jeriah."

Abraham laughed. "Surely you're not serious. You can't have married Lazy Jeriah. It's not possible. He has no job and begs off of anyone who will listen to him. He refuses to work for anything. How could the king allow such a thing?"

Mazel's cheeks began to burn red with embarrassment. Her husband was known as Lazy Jeriah, and Abraham confirmed what Mazel suspected: Jeriah didn't have any job or trade skills. "It was my father's idea. Excuse me, I have to go."

Mazel turned quickly and walked away. She liked Abraham and trusted him, but she didn't want him to see her so upset. Her father must have known Jeriah's reputation before he forced them into marriage. This was all part of his plan, and Mazel didn't know what she would do now.

Once Mazel gained her composure again, she found exactly what she needed and headed home. She was ready to be back in the quiet and solitude of her new home. She didn't want to chance running into somebody else she knew and having to explain her new life to them. She couldn't take the embarrassment.

When Mazel arrived back home, Jeriah was still sleeping. He had kicked his covers off and was snoring so loudly. It was already past noon, and he still hadn't gotten up for the day. "How can one man be so lazy?" she said to herself. But Mazel wasn't going to stand for this. She was used to being from sunrise to sunset.

Mazel went and filled a ceramic pitcher full of water from the nearby well and brought it back in. "Jeriah, wake up," she said. When he only grunted in reply, Mazel turned the pitcher over and soaked Jeriah in cold water.

He jumped up immediately and gasped for breath. When he realized where he was and what Mazel had done, he said, "What was that for?" If it had been someone other than the king's daughter, he would have given them an earful.

"It is past noon, and you need to get up. How can you sleep the day away?"

"It keeps my mind off of being hungry," he said.

Mazel hesitated. She didn't know what it was like to be hungry, but she had often seen the effects when she brought food down to the village for the poor. She had seen how eager the children were when they caught the scent of freshly baked bread. She was usually sympathetic toward them, but now she was torn between Jeriah's poor upbringing and his lazy nature. "Well, we have food that you can eat. Sleeping this long is unacceptable. We have work to do."

Jeriah groaned but found some food to begin eating; he didn't want to face whatever work Mazel had for him just yet.

Jeriah sat while he ate, but Mazel was so full of energy. She started to unpack all of the supplies she had just bought—wooden loom ,some rolls of colorful thick and thin wool yarn weft threads—and she laid them out so she could get to work immediately.

Jeriah couldn't hide his curiosity as he watched Mazel work. She was very precise and meticulous going through all of her goods. It was something Jeriah wasn't used to. "What is all of this for?" he asked finally.

Thinking Jeriah might actually get on board with this, Mazel lit up as she explained her idea of weaving a blanket to sell. "And you can take it down to the markets."

Mazel looked expectantly at him and thought he might be just as excited as she was. But Jeriah looked less than thrilled with her plan. Sitting around in a market stall all day trying to sell blankets to passersby didn't sound fun at all. It sounded like work. It would be hot, and he would have to talk to people. He wouldn't be able to slip a nap in.

Mazel could tell quickly that Jeriah was going to be difficult. How could she make a marriage with this man when her business idea was already starting to crumble? They needed to make money to eat, and he was already balking at it. She would just have to wait and see what would happen. If he didn't do a good enough job selling the blanket, then she would have to come up with something else.

Chapter Eight

It took a couple of days for Mazel to have enough blankets ready to sell. Every day, Jeriah slept until noon when Mazel would come in and dump water on his face. Then he would spend his afternoons sitting around and eating. He didn't offer to help Mazel in any way but would often complain about one thing or another.

When Mazel had enough blankets ready, she warned Jeriah the night before that he would need to get up early to walk into the city because they didn't have a horse. He would have to pull the cart laden with all of her work.

"Sure, I'll be up with the sun," Jeriah said with a laugh.

Mazel went into the room and locked the door behind her like she did every night, and Jeriah made up his bed on the floor in the front room. Jeriah went to bed laughing, thinking he would get the best of Mazel since she usually let him sleep until noon, but he was wrong.

As soon as the sun peaked over the horizon, Mazel was up and dressed. Of course, Jeriah was passed out and snoring on the floor. Mazel didn't hesitate as she went out to get some water and immediately poured the water all over him.

"It's still dark outside," Jeriah shouted while Mazel just stood there and smiled at him.

"You have a lot of work to do today. Might as well get an early start."

Jeriah grumbled as Mazel made breakfast for the two of them. It was the least she could after waking him so abruptly. Besides, she needed him to get into a better mood if he was going to do well at selling her blanket. She watched as he loaded the cart up with all of their goods, but before he started on his way down the dirt road, she said, "Could you buy a word from Sole today as well?"

"Who is Sole?" he asked as Mazel handed him a small coin.

"He's an intelligent person who shares ideas with people for one penny."

Jeriah took the penny, then headed down the road, and when he reached a crossing, he looked back. Mazel had turned to go back in the house already. Jeriah smiled, and rather than taking the road toward the city, he turned the other way and headed toward an orchard. He parked his cart under an apple tree and laid down in the shade.

Just because Mazel told him he needed to do something didn't mean he was just going to do it. She was his wife, if anything she should be listening to him and not the other way around. He didn't enjoy working, and he wasn't about to start. So Jeriah decided to spend the day under this tree, and then he would head home.

It was a long, relaxing day for Jeriah as he napped on and off and munched on apples he picked from the tree. When the sun began to set, he started pulling his cart back home. But then he remembered the penny Mazel had given him. He figured she would ask about visiting Sole, so he made the quick trip into town to find this man.

He found him at the edge of town. Most everyone had already gone home for the day, but Sole was sitting on a wooden armchair with a graving and seemed as though he had been waiting for Jeriah before he left as well. The man was old but didn't sit hunched over. He sat with his back straight and his head high.

Jeriah held out the penny. "I want to buy a word for today."

Sole carefully plucked the coin from Jeriah's hand and said, "Whoever your heart desires, that's the beauty."

"That's easy," Jeriah said and left without another word.

He was still trying to work out what his excuse for not having any money from sales would be when Mazel greeted him outside. She was practically jumping as she watched him walk up the drive.

"How did it go?" she called to him.

He didn't answer and tried to look as sad as possible as he pulled up by the house. Mazel looked in the back of the cart, and her face fell. It didn't look like he had sold anything.

"What happened?" she asked.

"It was very slow in the market today," Jeriah lied. "No one seemed to really be interested in what we have."

"Well, maybe tomorrow will be better," Mazel said as she led Jeriah inside. "Did you stop and speak with Sole?"

"Yes, he said, 'Whoever your heart desires, that's the beauty.'"

Mazel thought about it for a moment as she turned the phrase over in her mind. "That's a good lesson to learn."

She already had dinner ready and on the table. It was still warm, and Jeriah sat down to eat. Mazel was doing her best to stay positive and hoped that her attitude would be contagious. She didn't want to push Jeriah too much but knew that he wouldn't do anything on his own if he could help it. But she really believed he had done his best, so the next day when she sent him out again to another village, she expected to have better results. She also asked him to see Sole again.

But yet again, Jeriah returned with all of the blankets he had left with. Again, he said that it wasn't that busy in the marketplace and nobody was really interested in stopping by his stall to even look at their wares. He acted as though he had had a hard day of work though in reality he had just spend the whole day napping and eating like normal.

But he had gone to see Sole on his way home. Again, the old man was waiting for him as Jeriah passed him the penny. He said, "Where you eat your bread or open their house for you don't be uprooter."

Mazel was running out of supplies, so she made a quick trip into the nearest village. While there, she ran into Abraham again.

Abraham looked at her with concern, thinking about the last time he had seen her. "How have you been, Mazel?"

"All right," Mazel said as she looked through his goods.

Abraham was successful as a merchant, and she wished that Jeriah could learn a thing or two from him. That was when the idea hit her. "Could you do me a favor?"

"Anything for you," he said with a big smile.

"Could you teach Jeriah how to become a merchant? He's been going into different villages trying to sell my blankets, but he has not been successful. Every day he comes with as much as he left with. I don't know what else to do."

Abraham thought for a moment about it. "I could get my son to watch the stall tomorrow, and I can take Jeriah to the next village over. They usually have a lot of people early in the mornings."

"Oh, thank you so much, Abraham. I appreciate this a lot."

Jeriah went to bed that night expecting another easy day coming. He felt slightly bad about lying to Mazel. Eventually, she was going to find out what he was up to, but he figured he could get a couple more lazy days out of it before the rest of his life would be spent working.

The next morning, Jeriah actually woke up before Mazel dumped any water on him. Mazel saw this as a good sign that he was actually trying now. She had completed a few more bolts of blankets to sell and went to hand them to Jeriah. When she took a step toward him, her ankle turned hard, and she began to fall.

Jeriah moved quickly and was able to catch Mazel before she hit the ground. He cradled her in his arms, and their eyes locked for a moment. That was when Mazel saw something different in Jeriah. Before she had looked at him as a lazy vagrant, but now she saw a softer side. Jeriah also saw something else in Mazel's eye when he looked at her. He had never noticed just how beautiful she was, and by touching her, he had never felt before he could feel a definite connection and attraction there.

"Thank you," Mazel said as Jeriah eased her down into a chair.

Jeriah was about to say something when there was a knock on the door. He opened up the front door and saw Abraham standing there. Mazel made the quick introductions and apologized for not telling Jeriah last night that Abraham was coming over. "He's really successful, and he's going to show you how to be a merchant," Mazel said with a smile.

"Oh, great," Jeriah said as he plastered on a fake smile of his own. His easy day had just taken a wrong turn. There was no way for him to get out of this one.

Chapter Nine

The two men set out on the road, and this time, Jeriah wasn't able to pull off into the apple orchard again. He looked at it longingly as they passed by on their way to the next village over. Abraham was telling him some points on how to be a good merchant, but Jeriah wasn't really listening. He was still thinking about how beautiful Mazel's eyes were. He couldn't remember ever meeting someone with two different colored eyes.

As Jeriah andAbraham traveled to town to sell their goods, they saw a group of people near a well. There were clustered around the opening and talking. Some were yelling, others were crying, but most just looked confused. Jeriah andAbraham walked up to the group and looked in at the well.

"What is going on?" Jeriah asked.

A young man spoke up and said, "We need water, but we can't pull it from the well. Whoever goes down there, never comes back alive."

"We are so thirsty," a woman said. She had tear streaks down her cheeks and a small child clinging to her skirt.

Jeriah looked at the crowd for a moment and then turned to his partner. "I'll go in the well."

"Are you out of your mind?"Abraham asked. "You will die."

Jeriah was thinking about how he really didn't want to walk all the way into the village and spend all day trying to sell blankets. He figured it wouldn't be so bad going into the well. Surely everybody was exaggerating the danger. Besides, maybe if he did this, Mazel would look at him as more than just a lazy man. "I will take the chance."

Some of the people tried to stop him, but others encouraged him because they were so thirsty. They begged him to save their lives, so Jeriah made up his mind. He went down into the well with a bucket in hand. It was a long way to the bottom, and soon the light began to fade. He was plunged into darkness for a few minutes until he reached the very bottom. There was a strange light down there that he attributed to the sun's glare on the water.

At first, he didn't see anything amiss, but as soon as he bent down to scoop up some water, he heard someone behind him. When he turned around, he saw the most beautiful and terrifying creature he had ever seen.

From the waist up, this creature looked like a woman with long hair the color of gold. Her beasties long over the shoulder all the way half on her back. Her eyes were blue gray like pearls, which only added to her beauty. From the waist down, she blended in with the cave around her like a skirt, as if she were growing from the cave floor itself. The source of the light seemed to be coming from her.

"That is not your water to take," she said as her voice echoed around.

Jeriah took a few steps toward her. He hadn't even noticed that the well opened up into a cave when he first came down and was surprised to see the stalagmites and stalactites growing all around him. It was a terrifying site to behold, but as he moved closer to this frightening creature, he could see all of these mountains of jewels, gold, and fruit behind her.

"Who are you?" he asked. His voice came out stronger than he felt.

"My name is Jean," the creature said. "I will ask you one question. If you answer it correctly, then you may take some water and leave with your life. If you get it wrong, I will take your life." She pointed off to her right where the light barely touched. There, piled against a rough stone wall, were the bodies of all of the men who had come down before him.

Jeriah was too terrified to say anything, so he just nodded. He didn't have a choice.

Jean's terrible voice asked, "Which of these men is the one I choose? The handsomeathletic man, or the ordinary man with hazel eyes?"

“Whichever your heart desires,”Jeriah answered without hesitation. “You choose the ordinary guy.”

Jean was surprised because Jeriah was a normal man with a pure heart. She could see deep within his soul and could tell that he was more than what he appeared. She waved her hand to the side of the cave where there were many jewels, diamonds, and fruit. “You may take your pick,” she said.

Suddenly another creature came out from behind Jean.

“Beta will help you,” she said as she motioned toward the man.

He was a stooped figure who shuffled as he walked. Jeriah had to squint to get a good look, but he noticed this man Beta was twisted. His feet were turned around backward, which accounted for his shuffling. He was also bare-chested with no nipples and skin the color of fresh snow. Jeriah was terrified as he watched this creature move toward the pile of treasure.

Jeriah filled his bucket with water for the town. When he was done, Beta was standing right behind him, silent. He handed over a beautiful gold basket full of fruit. Jeriah had never seen this type of fruit before, and he wondered what they would taste like. He also knew that Mazel came from royalty, and jewels wouldn’t be that impressive to her. He thought she would enjoy the exotic food and the beautiful basket more than any of the jewels.

But before he left, a small ring caught his eye. It was unlike any he had ever seen before. It wasn’t a diamond, which was obvious. The stone at the center of the gold band seemed to be changing colors as he looked at it. One way it was red, the other way it was purple. He adjusted the basket in his arms so he could kneel down to pick up the ring. The way it changed colors made him think of Mazel with her exotic eyes, so he placed the ring in his pocket and left the cave.

When Jeriah came out of the well, the sun had already moved across the sky. It didn’t feel like he had been down in that well for so long, but it was almost dusk already. The crowd had only grown larger in his absence as word spread of his descent. They gathered around him as he pulled out of the well and raised a loud cheer.

“He’s done it,” one yelled while another shouted. “We’re saved.”

They passed the bucket around so everyone could get a drink. Though the bucket wasn’t all that large, there seemed to be just enough for everyone to get their fill though there were close to one hundred people gathered there.

“What was down there?” somebody asked when they noticed the basket Jeriah was carrying. Soon several people were looking at him expectantly.

"It was a terrible creature who asked me a question. If I got it wrong, she would have killed me. I don't recommend going down there."

He found Abraham who had been waiting all day for him and placed the basket on top of the blankets in the cart. He was anxious to get home and show his wife the basket. He wanted to tell her all about his adventure because maybe then she wouldn't see him as lazy anymore.

Chapter Ten

azel was waiting expectantly outside the front door again as the two men came up the drive. "How did it go?" she called.

This time she could see a smile on Jeriah's and Abraham's faces as they made their way to the house, but as they got closer, Mazel could see that yet again, none of the blankets had sold.

"What happened?" she asked.

"Let's go inside," Jeriah said as Abraham bid farewell and promised to come again the next morning. Jeriah picked up the basket and carried it into the house where he placed it on the table.

"Is this for me?" Mazel asked. Her eyes were wide, and she was smiling.

Jeriah told her all about his adventure that day and how he had won the fruit. "I had my pick of jewels and gold, but I thought you would appreciate the fruit more. It doesn't look like anything I've ever seen around here."

"They look beautiful and delicious," Mazel said.

They each reached in the basket to grab a piece of fruit at the same time, and their hands touched. They looked up at each other, and both could start seeing the magical love one another. For the first time since their marriage, Mazel wasn't eager to lock herself away in the bedroom. Instead, she stayed up with Jeriah, and they talked about their very different childhoods. Mazel went to bed feeling as though she were finally getting to know this man.

The next day, Jeriah woke up on his own once again. He was no longer dreading going to work because nothing he had to do would be as terrifying as when he faced Jean down in the well. And he didn't want to waste all of the improvements they had made in their relationship. Jeriah didn't want to let Mazel down.

In fact, Jeriah decided he was going to surprise Abraham by showing up at his house instead. Jeriah shaved and dressed in nice clothes. Mazel looked at him and couldn't believe how attractive he was. Jeriah leaned over and kissed her on the forehead. "I'll be back in a week. We need to go to a different town to sell all the blankets," he said.

Mazel blushed as he left.

While he was gone, Mazel cleaned the house and then turned her attention to the basket. It was so beautiful; she had never seen anything like it. But it also felt so heavy. She wasn't sure if it were the fruit or just the basket itself. She began looking at it further and moving the fruit around. That was when she saw it.

Underneath the fruit, there were hundreds of diamonds. She couldn't believe it. Mazel picked up a handful, and they sent a shower of rainbow prisms around the house when the light caught their facets. She let the diamonds of different sizes trickle through her fingers back into the bottom of the basket.

They were rich beyond belief. She grabbed a handful of the precious stones and put them in a small pouch. Then she moved the basket into a cabinet so it wouldn't be visible from the window. Mazel left the house and locked the door behind her.

When Jeriah arrived at Abraham's house, he knocked on the door, and Abraham's wife answered. Jeriah introduced himself, and she immediately smiled.

"Come in and have a seat. Abraham went to check on our shop to make sure our son will be able to handle it for a week while you both are gone. He should be back shortly."

Jeriah waited for about half an hour forAbraham to return home. When Abraham walked in the door and saw Jeriah sitting there talking with his wife, Abraham was surprised. Jeriah laughed at the look on Abraham's face.

"It's good to see you out and about so early," Abraham said as he greeted Jeriah.

"I figured it would surprise you."

Abraham said, "I'm just about ready to go. Let me get some money first."

Abraham went back into his bedroom where he normally kept his money. He liked to keep it hidden, just in case. But when he checked in his usual hiding spot, it was empty. Abraham moved some things around in an effort to find the money, but it was all gone. He felt betrayed, and only one suspect came to mind.

When Abraham came back to the front room, his face was grim. He leveled his gaze at Jeriah and asked directly, "Did you steal money from me?"

Jeriah was taken aback. He was completely shocked that Abraham would accuse him about stealing. "I would never steal from you. You have opened your heart and your family to me. I would never do that to a friend, especially after all you have done for me."

Abraham's wife stepped into the room at that moment; she had been listening in. "Abraham, I'm sorry, but I moved the money last night. I meant to tell you before bed, but you were so tired and fell asleep so fast that I didn't get a chance." She ran into the other room and came back with the money rolled together. It was all there.

Abraham's cheeks flamed red from embarrassment. He couldn't believe he had jumped to such a horrible conclusion about Jeriah. "I'm so sorry, Jeriah," he said. "I hope you can forgive me."

"Of course, I can forgive you. You are my friend."

The two men shook hands before they gathered their things and headed into town for a week. The awful incident was quickly forgotten.

After a long week of work , Jeriah arrived home. He had a good week and had sold most of the blankets he had taken into town. He had come to realize underAbraham's instruction that being a merchant wasn't as hard as he had made it out to be in his mind. He actually enjoyed talking with all of the people and showing off his wife's fine craftsmanship.

Abraham had commented, "You're a natural at convincing customers to buy your wares."

"Well, I spent most of my life on the street begging for food and clothing. I guess it was a good way to gain experience." Jeriah laughed.

As they were leaving the market, they passed a flower shop, and Jeriah couldn't help but buy a tulip that reminded him of Mazel's beauty. But he had a bigger surprise in store for her.

When he arrived at home, he tried to open the door, but it was locked. He was surprised and a little disappointed that Mazel wasn't out waiting for him like she had in the past. He figured Mazel was napping or busy with other work, so he knocked on the door. Instead of his beautiful wife, a large man he didn't recognize opened the door.

“What are you doing in my house?”Jeriah asked the man. “Are you Jeriah?”

“Yes.”

“You don’t live here anymore. Your wife gave this house to me and my family earlier today. I will show you where you live now.”

By the way my name is Joseph, thank you so much God bless you and your wife Mazel

Meanwhile, Jeriah, when he was following Joseph with a horse, was furious his heart was pounding, and he stopped hearing what Joseph was saying and thanking him nonstop for. Jeriah was terrified at what to expect,”Please, God. Just when I am starting to get close to Mazel...I don’t want to lose her too.”

Joseph continued explaining, “My house caught on fire. We were living with my kids on the street, and we didn’t know what we would have done without your help .Oh, we are almost here.”

Jeriah was in shock as the man directed him to a much larger house closer to the palace. It was bigger than any other house he had ever seen before. Mazel was standing in the doorway with a huge smile on her face as Jeriah walked up. “Come in,” she said. “I have so much to tell you.”

Jeriah was amazed when Mazel told him about the diamonds in the basket. He had no idea and couldn’t believe their good fortune. She then explained how she immediately went out and found a new house. After hearing the story of his childhood, she knew how much he disliked being in his old house and thought they needed a new start in their lives.

Jeriah then shared his good news about how well the business had gone that day. He sat her down at the table and enthusiastically explained everything he had learned fromAbraham. Jeriah was truly excited for work the next day. He wasn’t used to having a purpose to his life, but now Mazel was giving him that.

“We should invite my parents over,” Mazel said. “I wanted them to see how well we were doing.”

Mazel had sent them an invitation to visit but hadn’t said in the letter whom it was from. She wanted to surprise her mother and father with their good fortune. She knew there was already talk around the city about who had just moved into this lavish house, and surely the buzz had reached the palace. They would be intrigued by that alone, and they sent word that they would visit.

The king and queen arrived quickly to the new home. They were escorted to the guest room before seeing Mazel and Jeriah. They were overwhelmed with the beautiful and luxurious furnishings in the room. They had also been escorted by two guards, and the king couldn't help but wonder who their new neighbors could be.

Once they were done settling into their room, the guards returned to escort them to the main living area. They entered the large, open room, and the queen stopped dead in her tracks. Her hand flew up to her chest, and she whispered, "Mazel?"

"Yes, Mother. It's me," Mazel replied as she stepped forward and held her mother's outstretched hand.

"How?" was all that the king could say, so Mazel bid them to sit down and explained everything that had happened over the last several weeks.

They were happy that their daughter was doing so well. The king had to admit that he had been wrong about Jeriah after Mazel told him all about what went on in the well.

"Well, now that explains a lot," the king said. "I had a lord complaining to me about his village not being able to get water, and now I understand that this creature is the cause of it. I think it would be best if everyone just stayed away from that well." He then turned to his son-in-law. "Thank you, Jeriah, for being brave enough to face it and help out."

Jeriah graciously accepted the thanks then said, "But my name is actually Jeremiah. I didn't want to use my name because of my situation in life, but now I feel like I can finally use my given name." He was happy to be proving everyone wrong, but then he had another surprise in store. He got down on one knee and held out the closed tulip to Mazel. "I was forced to marry you by your father, but I don't regret it. I have fallen in love with you, and I give you this tulip as a sign that I want to remarry you, if you accept."

Mazel was smiling and took the tulip. As soon as she touched it, the tulip opened up, and inside the flower petals, there was a gorgeous shining ring. Mazel's eyes lit up as she marveled at the changing colors. She slipped it on her finger and said, "I have fallen in love with you after getting to know you. I accept."

They both had tears streaming down their cheeks as they kissed and embraced. The king and queen were also crying tears of joy. The king stood over the pair and said, "I give you my blessing. The queen and I are happy to leave the kingdom to the you both so you can produce the heir to the throne, and the royal line will continue"

"King ,call the Privy councillor,"

"Yes, Your Majesty" and he bowed down

"King, I want to do

"To announce for my future son-in-law Jeremiah and my daughter, Princess Mazel will be getting married again

I want to invite everyone in city and other Kingdoms to a ball.

Call the bishop to set the day for the wedding."

One month after preparations for the ball and wedding, Jeremiah and Mazel got married in church.

And they lived happily ever after.

Acknowledgments

It has always been my dream to write this book. Without Christina N.'s illustrations, I could not have brought this vision to life. I am deeply grateful to my parents, Daniel and Khatoun; my husband, Hovsep; my sister, Mayda; my brothers, Nerses and Toros; and to my family, friends, and readers for their unwavering support. Most of all, I give thanks to Jesus Christ.

www.ingramcontent.com/pod-product-compliance
Lightning Source LLC
Chambersburg PA
CBHW042117030726
47599CB00002B/254

* 9 7 8 1 9 7 0 6 1 7 5 2 8 *